P9-DEG-995

please, baby, please

by Spike Lee and Tonya Lewis Lee

illustrated by Kadir Nelson

SIMON & SCHUSTER BOOKS FOR YOUNG READERS

NEW YORK LONDON TORONTO SYDNEY SINGAPORE

SIMON & SCHUSTER BOOKS FOR YOUNG READERS

An imprint of Simon & Schuster's Children's Publishing Division

1230 Avenue of the Americas, New York, New York 10020

Book design by Dan Potash

The text for this book is sent in Alcoholica. The illustrations for this book are rendered in oils.

Printed in the United States of America

6 8 10 9 7

Library of Congress Cataloging-in-Publication Data

Lee, Spike.

Please, baby, please / by Spike Lee and Tonya Lewis Lee ; illustrated by Kadir Nelson.

p. cm.

Summary: A toddler's antics keep her mother busy as she tries to feed

her, watch her on the playground, give her a bath, and put her to bed.

ISBN 0-689-83233-8

[1. Toddlers—Fiction. 2. Mother and child—Fiction. 3. Afro-Americans—Fiction.]

I. Lee, Tonya Lewis. II. Nelson, Kadir, ill. III. Title.

PZ7.L514857 Pl 2001 [E]—dc21 99-462286

To Satchel and Jackson for all of
your curious creative energy.
Love,
Mommy and Daddy—S. L. and T. L. L.

For the ladies in my life, Keara, Amel, and Aya. I love you.
And for my dad, Lenwood Melvin Nelson, I love you and I miss you.—K. N.

Baby
by Keara Nelson

Go back to bed,
baby, please, baby, please.

Not on your HEAD,
baby baby baby, please!

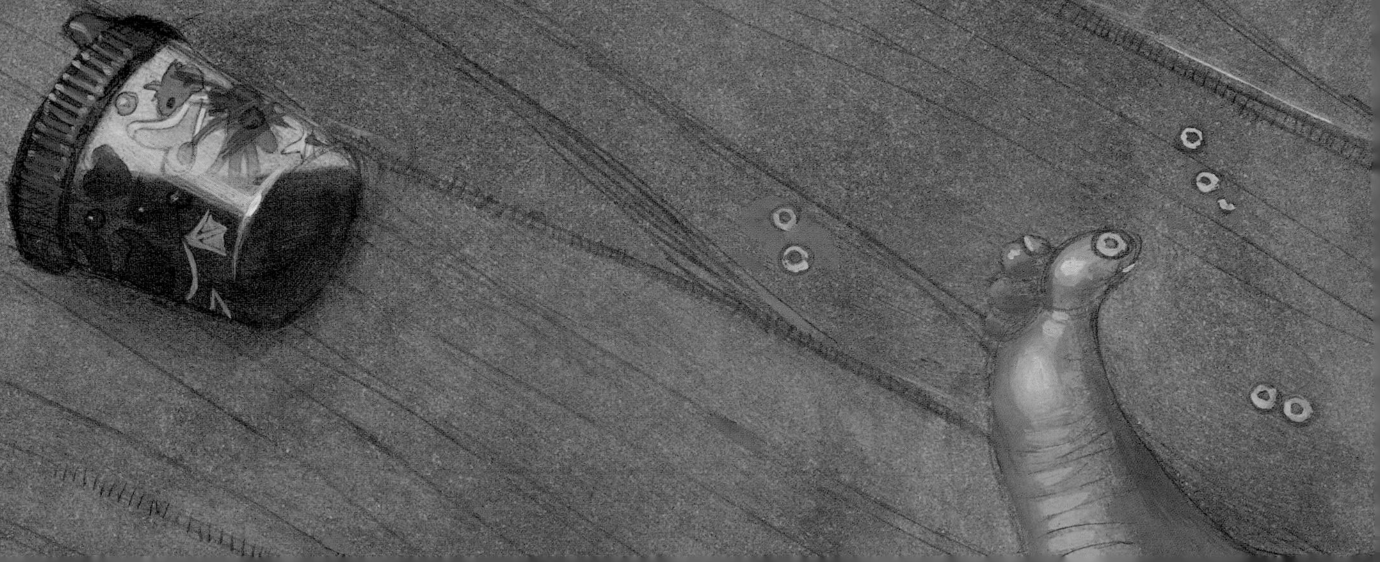

Keep off the wall,
baby baby, please, baby.

You share that ball,

please, baby baby baby.

Don't eat the sand,
baby baby baby, please.

Now hold my hand,
baby baby, please, baby.

It's time to go,
please, baby,
please.

Don't be so slow,
baby baby baby, please.

Please eat your peas,
baby baby
baby baby.

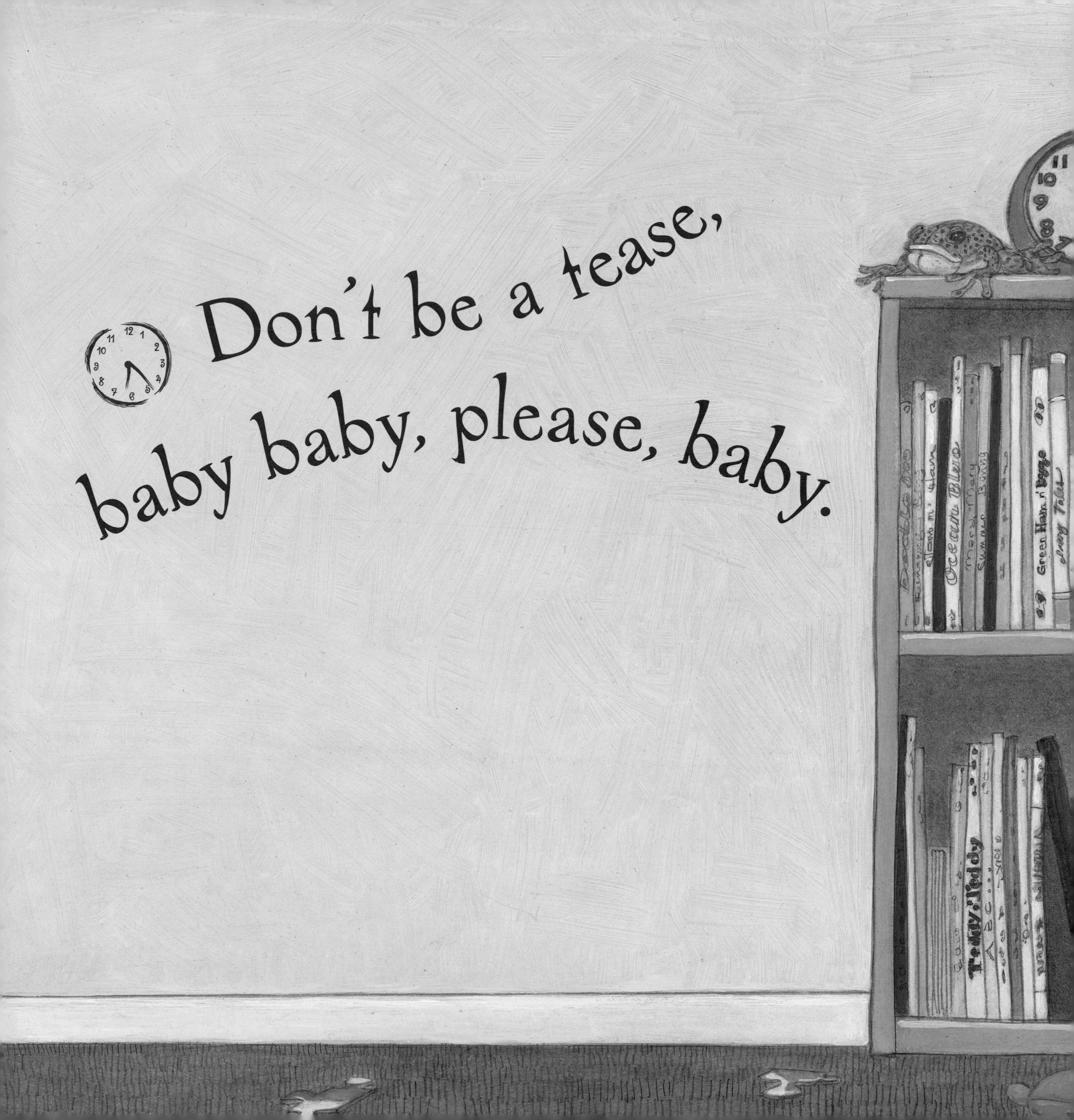

Don't be a tease,
baby baby, please, baby.

Please don't splash,
baby baby, please, baby!

NO! In the trash,
baby baby baby baby!

Now you
sleep tight,
please, baby,
please.

Kiss me good night?
Mama, Mama,
Mama, please.